NOT SO SPOOKY BOOK SERIES
BOOK ONE:

NOT SO SPOOKY HALLOWEEN

COLIN CHARLES NAUGHTON

PUBLISH AMERICA

PublishAmerica
Baltimore

First printing

ISBN: 9781462678563
PUBLISHED BY PUBLISHAMERICA, LLLP
www.publishamerica.com
Baltimore

Printed in the United States of America

There once was a little boy named Colin who was 6 years old and today is Halloween. Colin has been so excited about today that he has been wearing his costume for weeks preparing for this big day. Colin and his sister, Caitlyn who is 4 years old, also have been rummaging around through all different size and shaped bags making sure they had he biggest and best to fit all their candy they would get. Colin and his sister would even pretend they were out trick & treating, practicing saying "Trick or Treat" and planning their routes so they can get it perfect and the most candy.

Now the day is finally here. Colin was so excited about going out for Halloween he could hardly control himself. Colin's mom reminded him that he could not go out trick or treating until he finished all his homework and ate all of his dinner. So what did little Colin do? He ran and did all his homework making sure he dotted every little i and crossing all the t's. Once Colin finished his homework he then ran to the dinner table and sat down being the first one there making sure he ate every last crumb. Colin was not going to miss getting any candy tonight and wanted to get out there as fast as he could.

Colin's mom helped him and his little sister get their costumes on and said "now remember kids it's a Not So Spooky Halloween out there" and have fun. She then gave them each a big kiss and placed a flash light into Colin's pocket. Colin and his little sister ran out the door to meet their dad who was waiting for them ready to go.

Colin and his sister were going house to house, door bell to door bell saying trick or treat having such a fun time knowing all the candy they were getting. Darkness started rolling in quickly but that did not stop little Colin. He still went house to house even though his little sister was geting tired and could not keep up with him. So their daddy was staying back with his little sister letting Colin go ahead and collect more and more candy.

Then down the street near the end where it loops back around there was a spooky farm house with a large pumpkin field. In front of the pumpkin field there were three spooky Jack O' Lanterns that were glowing and seemed to look at and follow Colin. They were BIG and Orange and their eyes were glowing. Little Colin stopped and was scared. Colin looked back and could see his daddy with his little sister, but knew if he turned around to go back to them he would have to go in and Colin did not want to do that, he wanted to go on and get more candy and have fun. Colin remembered what his mother said then turned back around and looked at those three pumpkins and said" you're Not So Spooky" and he slowly started to walk by.

He made it by the first Jack O' Lantern and the second but then he spotted something in the corner of his eye. Colin STOPPED and turned slowly. There is saw right behind the Jack O 'Lanterns a SPOOKY scarecrow looking right at him. Colin yelled and ran back towards his father and sister. As Colin was running he again remembered what his mother said and STOPPED. He whipped around and started walking back towards the spooky scarecrow in the pumpkin patch. Colin was getting closer and closer to the pumpkin patch and the spooky scarecrow.

Colin kept saying "you're Not So Spooky, you're Not So Spooky" over and over as he walked closer and closer. Colin legs started to become weak and tremble as he was almost up to it. Then it moved and Colin froze and stared trembling and wanted to turn around to go to his daddy and sister. Colin dropped his candy bag and put his head down with his hands into his pockets and was about to turn and run when he felt something in his pocket. He started to feel it more and then he realized what it was. It was the flashlight his mom put into his pocket before they left. Colin quickly pulled it out and pushed the button to turn the flashlight on.

Colin turned and shined the light onto the pumpkin patch and he saw that the Jack O' Lanterns were Not So Spooky after all. Then Colin shined the flashlight onto the Spooky scarecrow and he saw that even the scarecrow was Not So Spooky either. As a matter of fact Colin could even now see that the scarecrow had a smile face on it. Colin started dancing around so happy saying" You're Not So Spooky and this is a Not So Spooky Halloween after all.

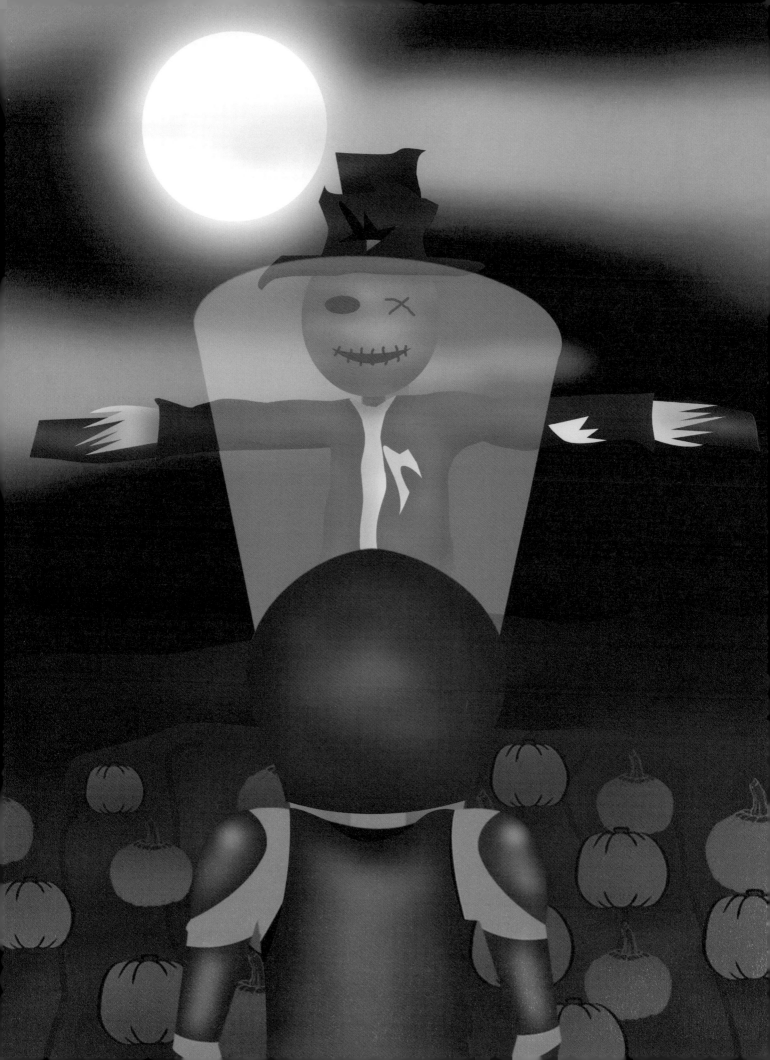

At that time his father and little sister had caught up to him and they asked Colin what was going on. Colin just smiled and said he was so happy and this was the best Halloween EVER. Colin then picked up his bag of candy and he continued on down the street with his flashlight on lighting the way so this Halloween will be NOT SO SPOOKY.

The end.

More children's book to come on the Not So Spooky book series:

Not So Spooky Nighttime. This children's book is about Colin going to bed by himself for the first time in his new room.

Not so Spooky Dentist Visit. This children's book is about Colin going to the dentist for the first time.

Not So Spooky Doctor's Visit. This Children's book is about Colin going to the doctors for a check up and shots.

Not So Spooky First Day to School. This is about Colin going to school.

An so on...This children's book series is so parents can read them these stories that kids can relate to and see that things in life are Not So Spooky after all.

CPSIA information can be obtained
at www.ICGtesting.com
Printed in the USA
LVIC04n1430170913
352857LV00032B

* 9 7 8 1 4 6 2 6 7 8 5 6 3 *